The Turkey Prince

RETOLD BY

Izzi Tooinsky

ILLUSTRATED BY

Edwina White

VIKING

VIKING

Published by the Penguin Group

Penguin Putnam Books for Young Readers, 345 Hudson Street, New York, New York 10014, U.S.A.

Penguin Books Ltd, 27 Wrights Lane, London W8 5TZ, England

Penguin Books Australia Ltd, Ringwood, Victoria, Australia

Penguin Books Canada Ltd, 10 Alcorn Avenue, Toronto, Ontario, Canada M4V 3B2

Penguin Books (N.Z.) Ltd, 182-190 Wairau Road, Auckland 10, New Zealand

Penguin Books Ltd, Registered Offices: Harmondsworth, Middlesex, England

First published in 2001 by Viking, a division of Penguin Putnam Books for Young Readers.

1 3 5 7 9 10 8 6 4 2

LIBRARY OF CONGRESS CATALOGING-IN-PUBLICATION DATA

Tooinsky, Izzi.

The turkey prince / retold by Izzi Tooinsky ; illustrated by Edwina White.

p.   cm.

Summary: A young prince who is afraid of becoming king decides that he is a turkey.

ISBN 0-670-88872-9 (hardcover)

[1. Princes—Fiction. 2. Self-confidence—Fiction.] I. White, Edwina, ill. II. Title.

PZ7.T635 Tu 2001

[E]—dc21   00-009292

Printed in Hong Kong

Set in Mrs. Eaves

The artwork for this book was created using acrylics, gouache, pencil, inks, tea,
and collage. The cover was executed on canvas with acrylics and inks.

Dedicated to the wisdom of children
—I. T.

All my love to Jarrah Moholy
with a good dose left for mankind at large
E. W.

Once in a far off kingdom, in a huge palace, in a busy kitchen, underneath the table next to the sink, there was a prince who would one day become king. But all was not right, for the prince had lost his mind and thought he was a turkey.

People say that one night at the palace there was a huge banquet. The king gave a speech, the queen told a story, and then the young prince was pushed onto the table and was expected to address the court. But instead . . .

he jumped off the table

and ran through the palace.

Then suddenly he threw off his velvet cape

and he ripped away his satin shirt.

He tore his silk pants to pieces
and yanked off his red socks.

He ran into the kitchen, squatted under the table, and
began to gobble like a turkey.

(*Now the young prince did not want to be a turkey. He did not choose to be a
turkey. But when he thought of himself leading and caring for the people, like his
father and mother did, it was very clear that he was a turkey, and a turkey cannot
be a king.*)

From that day forward he refused to leave the kitchen. He refused to wear any clothing, and he refused to eat any food except what was thrown onto the ground for him to peck at.

The king and queen were frantic. They called physicians and nurses, sages and monks. These people applied green-colored lotions and bad-smelling potions. They chanted and prayed. But not one of them knew how to cure the Turkey Prince.

One day an unknown healer came to the castle. His clothes were shabby, but his face glowed like a new star.

With a bold smile and a ridiculous bow he asked the king and queen, "May I attempt to cure the Turkey Prince?"

The healer was led to the kitchen. He tiptoed to the corner
and took a seat, where for two days he merely observed the
strange and lonely life of the Turkey Prince.

On the third day, to the great astonishment
of everyone in the castle, the healer howled
and shrieked.

He threw off his shirt,

kicked off his pants, and
squatted next to the prince.

No one was more surprised than the young prince himself.
He hid behind a table leg and stared at this wild stranger.
Finally the prince spoke. "Just who do you think you are?"
he sputtered, "and what right do you have to be here?"
The healer turned to the prince and answered slowly, "I'm
surprised you can't tell. I'm a turkey, just like you."

The prince looked the stranger up and down. A smile spread across his face. "How wonderful. I guess it's true. You are a turkey, too." And the two talked and sang under that table long into the night. The king and queen watched from the doorway, and they were delighted to see their son at ease again, even if he still thought he was a turkey.

Day by day the healer watched as the prince became more relaxed and less frightened.

One chilly night the healer nudged the prince and said, "Watch this." Then he stood up and slipped on a warm furry coat.

The prince was shocked. He squawked, "What are you doing? You're a turkey, yet you are putting on clothes just like a human."

The healer answered slowly, "I am not confused. I know who I am. I am a turkey who is cold, and I am going to wear this coat. Why shouldn't I?"

And the prince thought, "Could a turkey who is cold wear a coat? Of course, why not?" The chilly prince clumsily climbed out from underneath the table and also dressed himself in a long warm coat.

Then one afternoon, the healer nudged the boy again and smiled. "I'm starved, and they are not going to throw us grain until the morning. Let's go get some bread and cheese." He walked to the counter, cut a large piece of rye bread, laid a slice of yellow cheese on it, and began to chew with delight.

The prince screeched, "What? You are a turkey, but here you are eating just like a person."

The healer looked him in the eye and answered slowly, "I am not confused. I know who I am. I am a turkey who loves the taste of this food, so I'm going to eat it. Why shouldn't I?"

And once again the prince reasoned, "I am a turkey, too, and I also love bread and cheese, so why not eat it?" So the prince began to enjoy his meals again, like any child his age.

Little by little the two friends began
exploring the world beyond the kitchen.
Although the prince was afraid, he
followed the healer through the
gates of the palace and into the
streets and alleyways of the
kingdom.

There he saw people laughing and he saw others crying. He saw newborns and old people. He saw wealth and he saw poverty. He saw people who were healthy and others who were sick and dying.

The two traveled to distant lands and across blue oceans to hot green jungles. The prince learned how to build bridges across wild rivers, how to locate sweet water in the desert, and how to find a real smile on a sad child's face. He grew more confident each passing day.

After they returned from their journey, the healer made a special visit to the royal family. With a bold smile and ridiculous bow he told them, "The prince loves his life again. My job is finished here. I must move on."

He was given a new coat, a fine hat, a bag of gold, and all the gratitude a family can give.

The wheel of time turned until the old king and queen died and were laid to rest. The prince then became the new monarch of the land. He ruled wisely and was loved and respected by his people.

Frequently he would stroll through his kingdom, stopping in villages and towns to speak with his beloved subjects.

One day, as he spoke to a large group, he noticed a very sad man and woman at the edge of the crowd. He approached them and asked, "Is there some way that I might be of assistance to you?" The husband's face lit up with hope, but despair filled his wife's eyes. The woman answered, "Oh your highness, I wish you could, but our troubles are beyond help. You see, we have a little boy, and he thinks . . . he's a turkey."

"Take me to the child at once," demanded the king.

In the kitchen, underneath the table, next to the sink, was the little boy. With a look of crazy wisdom in his eyes, the king tossed off his crown, he dropped his velvet cape, and he squatted down. The amazed boy stared in disbelief, and then, for the first time in years, he spoke.

"Just who do you think you are?" he sputtered, "and what right do you have to be here?"

"I'm surprised you can't tell," said the king gently. "I'm a turkey, just like you."